My Fabulous Friends

By Mary Man-Kong

A Random House PICTUREBACK® Book
Random House 🏠 New York

Published in the United States by Random House Children's Books, a division of Random House, Inc.,
1745 Broadway, New York, NY 10019, and in Canada by Random House of Canada Limited, Toronto.
No part of this book may be reproduced or copied in any form without permission from the copyright owner.
Pictureback, Random House, and the Random House colophon are registered trademarks of Random House, Inc.
Library of Congress Control Number: 2009904824   ISBN: 978-0-375-85789-8
www.randomhouse.com/kids   Printed in the United States of America   10 9 8 7 6 5 4 3 2 1

Barbie

Barbie is a movie star! She enjoys playing different roles in all her films. From a fairy to a princess to a mermaid, Barbie can do it all!

Being a star is a lot of fun—and Barbie loves to shine on the red carpet!

Barbie's Dream House

After working on movie sets all day, Barbie loves to come home. Her house is cool and fun and has everything a girl could want—even a slide to the pool!

Barbie especially likes her house because she can hang out and share it with . . .

Teresa

Teresa is one of Barbie's best friends. She is very artistic and her designs are *hot*!

Nikki

Nikki is another one of Barbie's best friends. Honest and bold, she isn't afraid to tell it like it is. Nikki is a great dancer and practices new routines with Barbie all the time.

The scoreboard reads: 01 00 *Barbie*

Summer

Summer is super-sporty. Barbie and Summer love camping and playing tennis together. Summer is always on the go—and ready for adventure!

Raquelle

Raquelle is an actress, too. She competes with Barbie for roles and always has to wear the latest fashions first.

Ken

Ken is cool, charming, and kind. He is the captain of the football team and is totally into sports.

Barbie & Ken

Barbie likes Ken a lot—and he's the first person she would ask to a premiere.

Ryan

Ryan is sooo cute! He's one of the coolest boys at school, but he's a little mysterious. All the girls want to talk to him—and find out more about him!

Steven

Steven is Ken's best friend. He is very funny and loves all the latest techno-gadgets and gear. Steven loves to tease Ken about liking Barbie, but he secretly has a crush on Nikki.

Blissa

Blissa, Barbie's cat, loves being treated like a princess, so Barbie gave her a tiara. Blissa is so cute and cuddly—she's *purr*-fect!

Lacey

They say a dog is a man's best friend. Well, a dog can be a girl's best friend, too! Lacey is Barbie's cute little Chihuahua. Lacey loves to play hide-and-seek with Barbie.

Sequin

Sequin is Barbie's pet poodle. Sequin loves wearing pretty jeweled collars so she can sparkle and shine!

Barbie's Friends

Each of Barbie's friends is different in his or her own way—that's what makes them so special! They are all fun and fabulous, too—just like Barbie!